# THE TOOTH FAIRY

# TOOTH BE TOLD

### Adapted by Sonia Sander

**SCHOLASTIC INC.**
New York    Toronto    London    Auckland
Sydney    Mexico City    New Delhi    Hong Kong

ISBN-13: 978-0-545-16818-2
ISBN-10: 0-545-16818-X

12 11 10 9 8 7 6 5 4 3 2 1          9 10 11 12 13/0

Printed in the U.S.A.          23
First printing, December 2009

Life as a hockey player is tough . . . but it's not nearly as hard as being the Tooth Fairy.

My fans call me the Tooth Fairy because I'm great at knocking out teeth in the hockey rink.

As it turns out, I'm also great at destroying kids' dreams with my bad attitude . . . and someone decided to teach me a lesson. I was turned into an actual tooth fairy!

Given my talent with teeth, I was sure life as the real tooth fairy would be a piece of cake.

Boy, was I wrong.

For starters, my uniform didn't come close to fitting right.

And even when my uniform was fixed,
it just wasn't my style.

I was used to hockey equipment, not fairy supplies.

A fairy named Jerry gave me a tool pouch with shrinking paste, barking mints, and even amnesia dust inside.

I was sure that flying across the ice would help me fly through the air.

Once again, I was very wrong.

Flight training was dizzying — and painful!

I thought flying was the toughest part — until I had my first case. I decided to use my shrinking paste.

It was hard work to get inside the house carrying a whole dollar!

Then, when I woke up the kid, I knew I was in trouble.

I didn't want the same thing to happen on my next case.

So that time, I used a little amnesia dust to help me.

The problem was, I used a little too much.

The family couldn't remember who
they were!

This tooth fairy thing just wasn't for me,
and my hockey skills were suffering, too.
But I wasn't allowed to give up!

Using the shrinking paste and the amnesia dust wasn't working.

So I thought I'd try being invisible.

That didn't work either. I ended up scaring the family!

Needless to say, I was in trouble with my boss, Lily. She was pretty angry with me!

I guess the dog hanging off my wing didn't help.

To make matters worse, I ran out of
fairy supplies!

Luckily, I made a friend in Ziggy.
He helped me get some extra supplies.

At least, I thought he'd helped me —
until I tried some of the supplies.

They didn't work quite right.

Boy, was I in for a bad night!

I decided if I was going to do the job right, I had to do it my way. That meant dressing the part.

Things were going much better already!
I used amnesia powder on the dad at
the next house, before he could even
get scared.

Things were going better on the ice, too.

With some practice, I was back to being one of the Ice Wolves' star players!

I was sure my next case would be a breeze,
but then I found out it was Gabe's room.

He was the kid whose dreams I had
crushed when he'd told me he wanted
to be a hockey player, too.

I knew I had to make it up to him, so I left him some extra money.

But that wasn't enough. I had to make him believe again.

I just hoped my note would do the trick.

**Not every case is going to be perfect.**

**But you can't beat the feeling of helping a kid's dreams come true!**

It doesn't take much to ruin a kid's dreams, but helping kids believe again is a full-time job.

So it doesn't hurt to have a little fairy
magic on your side!